For Anjali. Never stop questioning. JR

For Avi. Adventures await. AW

Library of Congress Cataloging-in-Publication Data
Rustgi, Jennifer, author. | White, Ashley, 1984- illustrator.
moon of my own / by Jennifer Rustgi ; illustrated by Ashley White.
tion: First edition. | Nevada City, CA : Dawn Publications, [2016] |
nary: "A young girl travels the world in a dream with her faithful
anion, the moon, showing moon phases from iconic places on all seven
nents. Includes resources and activities for teachers and facts about
noon and the places visited"-- Provided by publisher.
ers: LCCN 2016000274| ISBN 9781584695721 (hardback) | ISBN
584695738 (pbk.)
s: | CYAC: Moon--Fiction.
cation: LCC PZ7.1.R88 Mo 2016 | DDC [E]--dc23 LC record available at
ccn.loc.gov/2016000274

ress and computer production — Patty Arnold, *Menagerie Design & Publishing*

Manufactured by Regent Publishing Services, Hong Kong
Printed May, 2016, in ShenZhen, Guangdong, China
10 9 8 7 6 5 4 3 2 1
First Edition

A MOO
OF MY

By Jennifer Rustgi ▴ Illustrated by Ashley White

Dawn Publications